THIS BOOK BELONGS TO:

_____

_____

_____

To my children, Ryan and Anna

GREAT ART STARTS WITH
JUST A SCRIBBLE.

THIS IS A STORY ABOUT SCRIBBLE,
WHOSE LINES WOULD CROSS AND WIGGLE.

TINY LOOPS WOULD START HIM SMALL.
BIGGER SWIRLS WOULD MAKE HIM TALL.

He could be shades of green or baby blue,
even crazy colors ... he loved them too!

CHOOSING BRIGHT COLORS MADE HIM FEEL FREE,
YOU NEVER KNEW WHICH ONE HE WOULD BE.

THEN ONE DAY, SCRIBBLE TOOK A SHORT WALK,
WHERE HE FOUND A HOUSE AND STOPPED TO TALK.
"HELLO," SAID SCRIBBLE, "IT'S SUCH A GREAT DAY,
I THOUGHT I'D COME OVER AND WE COULD ALL PLAY."

THE HOUSE NEVER SAW ANYTHING LIKE SCRIBBLE BEFORE.
BUT HE WAS CURIOUS ENOUGH, TO FIND OUT A BIT MORE.
SO, EVEN THOUGH HE WAS GRUMPY AND DIDN'T WANT TO PLAY,
HE STILL MANAGED TO GRUNT, "WHAT ARE YOU ANYWAY?"

SCRIBBLE WAS CONFUSED AND DIDN'T KNOW WHAT TO SAY.
SO HE SAID TO THE HOUSE, "I'M JUST A SCRIBBLE ... IS THAT OKAY?"

"IT'S NOT OKAY," SAID THE HOUSE, "YOU DON'T LOOK RIGHT.
YOUR LINES AREN'T STRAIGHT AND YOUR COLORS ARE TOO BRIGHT."

"But color is fun," Scribble said, "I can show you why.
Just give me a chance. Please let me try."

"NO!" SAID THE HOUSE, "YOU CANNOT STAY.
YOU'RE NOTHING LIKE ME. NOW GO AWAY!"

Hearing those words made Scribble so sad.
A tear ran down his face. He felt really bad.

"BUT I WON'T BE UPSET," HE PROCLAIMED THAT DAY.
SO, HE CHANGED HIS COLORS AND WENT ON HIS WAY.

He continued his walk and soon found the sun.
Along with the clouds, they could all have some fun!

BUT THE SUN SAW HIM COMING AND TOLD HIM TO STOP.
"YOUR LINES ARE TOO MESSY, AND WE DON'T HAVE A MOP!
TURN AROUND, LITTLE SCRIBBLE," HE WENT ON TO SAY.
"GO BACK TO YOUR HOME ... PLEASE JUST GO AWAY!"

"BUT YOU'RE NOT BEING NICE!" SCRIBBLE SHOUTED, QUITE MAD.
"THE FACT THAT I'M DIFFERENT DOESN'T MAKE ME SO BAD.
MY COLORS ARE SPECIAL, AND MY LINES ARE JUST FINE.
IF YOU'D GIVE ME A CHANCE, WE COULD HAVE A GREAT TIME!"

"SHOULD WE ASK HIM TO PLAY?" THEY HUDDLED TO DISCUSS.
"IT'S FUN WITH MORE FRIENDS, IT'S USUALLY JUST US."
AND ALTHOUGH THEY WERE WORRIED THIS WOULDN'T WORK OUT,
BEING MEAN TO SCRIBBLE WASN'T WHAT THEY WERE ABOUT.

SCRIBBLE WAS SURPRISED AT WHAT HE SAW THE NEXT DAY.
ALL THE DRAWINGS WERE THERE AND THEY WANTED TO PLAY.
EVEN RAINBOW SHOWED UP AND HE NEVER CAME BY,
HE WAS STANDING RIGHT THERE, NEAR THE SUN IN THE SKY.

"WE'RE SO SORRY," SAID THE CLOUDS, AS THEY HELD BACK THEIR TEARS.
"PLEASE COME PLAY," SAID THE HOUSE, "WE HAVEN'T HAD FUN IN YEARS."

"I FORGIVE YOU!" SCRIBBLE SHOUTED, AS HE DID A HAPPY DANCE.

THEY WERE SO GRATEFUL HE GAVE THEM ANOTHER CHANCE.

SCRIBBLE GATHERED UP HIS COLORS AND PLAYED WITH EVERYONE.

BLUE, PURPLE, GREEN, AND YELLOW...IT WAS ALL SO MUCH FUN!

LOOK WHAT THEY CREATED WHEN THEY FINALLY CAME TOGETHER..

THE ART WAS SO BEAUTIFUL, AND IT WAS BETTER THAN EVER!

SPECIAL THANKS!

A special thank you goes out to my wonderful husband, to my two children who inspired me to create this book, and to everyone who helped and supported me during this process!

I'm NOT just a Scribble... highlights the importance of inclusiveness while also providing a unique perspective on children's art. I'm hoping that each child who is read this book will express their individuality and creativity through their art, even if they think, "I can't draw." Sometimes all it takes to start the art process is a little encouragement and a little scribble!

I want to give a special shout out to kindergarten and preschool teachers, some of the most incredible people I've met through this experience. Their encouragement and excitement for this book has been truly inspirational.

After you read *I'm NOT Just a Scribble...*, I encourage you to share your children's scribble art on social media @imnotjustascribble and #ScribbleStickerArt, as I believe it is the start of something amazing!

#ScribbleStickerArt